R0068174911

12/2012

# Make a Trade, Charlie Brown!

## Visit us at www.abdopublishing.com

Reinforced library bound edition published in 2011 by Spotlight, a division of ABDO Publishing Group, 8000 West 78th Street, Edina, Minnesota 55439. This edition was reprinted by permission of United Feature Syndicate, Inc.

Printed in the United States of America, North Mankato, Minnesota.
092010
012011
This book contains at least 10% recycled materials.

## Library of Congress Cataloging-in-Publication Data

This title was previously cataloged with the following information:

Alfonsi, Alice.
  Make a trade, Charlie Brown! / by Charles M. Schulz; adapted by Alice Alfonsi.
    p. cm. — (Peanuts ready-to-read)
  "Based on the television special produced by Lee Mendelson and Bill Melendez."
  Summary: Charlie Brown wants so much to win a baseball game that he tries to trade Lucy, his worst player, and even considers trading Snoopy.
  [1. Baseball—Fiction. 2. Loyalty—Fiction.] I. Schulz, Charles M. ill. II. Title. III. Series.
  PZ7.A3842Mak 2004
  [E]—dc22                                      2003013182

ISBN: 978-1-59961-806-7 (reinforced library bound edition)

All Spotlight books have reinforced library bindings and are manufactured in the United States of America.

# Make a Trade, Charlie Brown!

Based on the comic strips
by Charles M. Schulz
Adapted by Darice Bailer
Art adapted by Peter and Nick LoBianco

Ready-to-Read

Little Simon

New York   London   Toronto   Sydney   Singapore

The last snow of winter was falling in the park but Charlie Brown didn't care. He was dreaming of summer and baseball.

"Why are you out here?" asked Linus.

"Memories," said Charlie Brown, sighing. "Some of my happiest memories were made here."

"But what about all the games we lost?" Linus asked.

"That was because of Lucy!" Charlie Brown cried. "She must be the worst right fielder in the history of baseball!"

"Are we going to have a baseball team this year?" Lucy asked.

"Yes," said Charlie Brown, "but we weren't going to tell you because we all know you are the worst player in the history of the game."

"Put me down for right field," said Lucy.

Charlie Brown sighed.

Spring arrived, and Charlie Brown's thoughts turned to baseball. He decided to try and coach Lucy. He wanted her to be a better player. Most of all, Charlie Brown wanted to win.

"I'm going to hit a fly ball," he said to Lucy. "Try to catch it and throw it back."

CRACK! The ball flew high into the sky.

"Catch it, Lucy!" Charlie Brown cried.

Lucy waited for the ball to come down. She tried to catch it but missed. The ball landed in the bushes. Lucy searched for the ball but didn't find it. Finally she picked up the whole bush and brought it to Charlie Brown.

"It's in here someplace," she said.

"Lucy is a terrible right fielder!"
Charlie Brown cried. "She doesn't have
the skills to win."

"What skills does an outfielder need?"
Linus asked.

"Good eyes and a good throwing arm,"
said Charlie Brown.

Snoopy raced past them.
CLOMP! He caught a fly ball
in his mouth.

Charlie Brown added, "And
a good set of teeth."

By mid-season, things were very bad. Charlie Brown's team had lost every game. He felt like a terrible manager.

"I've made a decision," Charlie Brown said. "I'm going to trade some players. A few trades can make our team better."

"That's a great idea," said Lucy. "Why don't you trade yourself?"

Charlie Brown called Peppermint Patty.
"Do you want to trade a few players?"
he asked.

"I don't know, Chuck," said Patty.
"The only good player you have is the
little kid with the big nose!"

"You mean Snoopy?" Charlie Brown
asked. "Oh no, I could never trade him.
I was thinking more of Lucy." Charlie
Brown heard a click and a dial tone.
Peppermint Patty had hung up!

"How are your baseball trades coming?" Linus asked.

"Terrible," Charlie Brown said. "Peppermint Patty wants Snoopy. I told her no, but maybe I was wrong."

Linus frowned and said, "You mean you would trade your own dog just to win a few ball games?"

"Win!" Charlie Brown sighed. Then he smiled. "What a wonderful word. Win." Charlie Brown ran to the phone and called Peppermint Patty. "I've decided to trade Snoopy," he said.

"That's great!" Peppermint Patty cried. "I'll give you five players for Snoopy."

"Uh . . . okay . . . fine," Charlie Brown said. But when he hung up the phone, he had second thoughts. "What have I done?" he cried. "I've traded my own dog! I've become a *real* manager!"

Charlie Brown went outside to see Snoopy. "This is a hard thing for me to say," he said. "I've traded you to Peppermint Patty for five new players."

"Give me a sign," Charlie Brown told Snoopy. "A sign that you don't hate me."

"BLEAH!" said Snoopy.

"That was not what I wanted to hear!" Charlie Brown cried.

Schroeder was angry with Charlie Brown. He thought trading Snoopy was stupid.

"He's your own dog!" Schroeder said. "Does winning a ball game mean that much to you?"

"I don't know," said Charlie Brown. "I have never won a ball game."

Linus was angry too.

"I'm so disappointed in you," Linus said, "that I don't even want to talk to you. And stop breathing on my blanket!"

Soon Charlie Brown was a nervous wreck.

"Good grief!" he cried. "I've made a terrible mistake."

"I was wrong," Charlie Brown said. "The thought of possibly winning a few ball games blinded me to the duty I have to love and protect my dog."

Charlie Brown raced up to Snoopy. "Look!" he cried. "I'm tearing up the contract. The trade is off."

"Thanks, Chuck," said Peppermint Patty. "Those players I traded said they would give up baseball before they would play on *your* team."

"I'm crushed," said Charlie Brown. But he didn't really mean it. He was glad to have Snoopy back on his team again. Snoopy was happy too!

By the next game Charlie Brown was
frustrated again. "We can not win this
game with Lucy out there in right field,"
he said.

"What will you do?" Schroeder asked.

"I've got an idea!" said Charlie Brown.

"Go home," Charlie Brown told Lucy. "Sit in the kitchen and have a glass of lemonade. I'll pitch the ball so they will hit it into the kitchen. You can catch it there."

Lucy went home and sat in the kitchen for a long, long time. "I think he tricked me," she said.

Peppermint Patty had troubles too. Her right fielder was as bad as Lucy.

"Why do I have to play right field?" said Marcie.

"It's tradition," Peppermint Patty replied. "The worst player *always* plays right field."

"I hate baseball!" yelled Marcie.

Peppermint Patty called Charlie Brown. "Chuck! Let's trade right fielders."

"Great!" Charlie cried. "I'd trade Lucy for *anyone!*"

When Lucy found out, she was angry. "You traded *me* for that stupid girl with glasses?" Lucy cried. "You were robbed!"

"No. I got the better deal," Charlie Brown told her. "Peppermint Patty threw in a pizza, too."

At her first game on Charlie's team,
Marcie never left the pitcher's mound.
It made playing baseball hard for
Charlie Brown.

"Shouldn't you be out in right field?"
he asked.

"I hate baseball," Marcie said. "I am
only playing because I've always been
fond of you."

Lucy wasn't working out for Peppermint Patty either.

"Keep your eye on the ball!" Peppermint Patty told her.

Lucy walked up to the mound and stared at the ball as Peppermint Patty tried to pitch.

"That's hard to do when you keep moving it around," said Lucy.

Peppermint Patty screamed, "Get back out to right field where you belong!"

"The trade is off," Peppermint Patty told Charlie Brown. "Lucy is the worst player I have ever seen. You need to take her back."

"But I already ate the pizza!" said Charlie Brown.

The next day Lucy was out in right field under an umbrella. When a ball was blasted to her it bounced off the umbrella and fell to the ground.

"It's not even raining," shouted Charlie Brown. "Hey, where is everybody going?"

Suddenly thunder crashed and the rain poured down. Charlie Brown sighed. "It's just a little rain," he said.